Astrosaurs

THE CLAWS OF CHRISTMAS

Steve Cole

Illustrated by Woody Fox

RED FOX

THE CLAWS OF CHRISTMAS
A RED FOX BOOK 978 1 862 30253 2

First published in Great Britain by Red Fox,
an imprint of Random House Children's Books
A Random House Group Company

This edition published 2007

1 3 5 7 9 10 8 6 4 2

Text copyright © Steve Cole, 2007
Cover illustration and map © Charlie Fowkes, 2007
Illustrations copyright © Woody Fox, 2007

The Random House Group Limited makes every effort to ensure that the
papers used in its books are made from trees that have been legally
sourced from well-managed and credibly certified forests. Our paper
procurement policy can be found at: www.randomhouse.co.uk/paper.htm

Mixed Sources
Product group from well-managed
forests and other controlled sources
www.fsc.org Cert no. TT-COC-2139
© 1996 Forest Stewardship Council

Typeset in Bembo Schoolbook by Palimpsest Book Production Limited,
Grangemouth, Stirlingshire

Red Fox Books are published by Random House Children's Books,
61–63 Uxbridge Road, London W5 5SA

www.**kids**at**random**house.co.uk

Addresses for companies within The Random House Group Limited
can be found at: www.randomhouse.co.uk/offices.htm

THE RANDOM HOUSE GROUP Limited Reg. No. 954009

A CIP catalogue record for this book is available from the British Library.

Printed in the UK by CPI Bookmarque, Croydon, CR0 4TD

For Freddie Hill

WARNING!

THINK YOU KNOW ABOUT DINOSAURS?

THINK AGAIN!

The dinosaurs . . .

Big, stupid, lumbering reptiles. Right?

All they did was eat, sleep and roar a bit. Right?

Died out millions of years ago when a big meteor struck the Earth. Right?

Wrong!

The dinosaurs weren't stupid. They may have had small brains, but they used them well. They had big thoughts and big dreams.

By the time the meteor hit, the last dinosaurs had already left Earth for ever. Some breeds had discovered how to travel through space as early as the Triassic period, and were already enjoying a new life among the stars. No one has found evidence of dinosaur technology yet. But the first fossil bones were only unearthed in 1822, and new finds are being made all the time.

The proof is out there, buried in the ground.

And the dinosaurs live on, way out in space, even now. They've settled down in a place they call the Jurassic Quadrant and over the last sixty-five million years they've gone on evolving.

The dinosaurs we'll be meeting are

 part of a special group called the Dinosaur Space Service. Their job is to explore space, to go on exciting missions and to fight evil and protect the innocent!

These heroic herbivores are not just dinosaurs.

They are *astrosaurs*!

NOTE: The following story has been translated from secret Dinosaur Space Service records. Earthling dinosaur names are used throughout, although some changes have been made for easy reading.

THE CREW OF THE DSS SAUROPOD

**CAPTAIN
TEGGS STEGOSAUR**

ARX ORANO,
FIRST OFFICER

GIPSY SAURINE,
COMMUNICATIONS
OFFICER

IGGY TOOTH,
CHIEF ENGINEER

Jurassic Quadrant

Ankylos

Steggos

Diplox

INDEPENDE
DINOSAU
ALLIANC

vegetarian
sector

Squawk
Major

DSS
UNION OF
PLANETS

PTEROSAURI

Tri System

Corytho

Lambeos

Iguanos

Aqua Minor

Geldos Cluster

Teerex Major

Olympus

TYRANNOSAUR
TERRITORIES

Planet Sixty

Raptos

THEROPOD EMPIRE

Megalos

Cryptos

vegmeat
zone
(neutral space)

SEA REPTILE
SPACE

Pliosaur
Nurseries

Not to scale

THE
CLAWS
OF
CHRISTMAS

Chapter One

THE SHOWER OF GIFTS

"Tomorrow is Christmas Eve!" cried
Captain Teggs Stegosaur.
"I can't wait for our
Christmas holidays
to begin!" He
hung a bauble on
the tree in the
control room of
his spaceship – and
then ate the bottom
branch!

"Captain!" said Gipsy, flicking him
with a piece of tinsel – she was a
stripy hadrosaur, in charge of the ship's
communications. "You keep eating the

Christmas trees before
I can finish
decorating
them!"
Teggs
grinned.
"Sorry,
Gipsy. I
always feel
extra-hungry
at Christmas!"

In fact, being an eight-ton
stegosaurus, Teggs felt extra-hungry
most of the time. He was in charge of
the DSS *Sauropod*, the finest vessel in
the Dinosaur Space Service, and going
on exciting adventures the whole time
was a hungry business.

Right now, the *Sauropod* was taking
them back to DSS Headquarters for a
Christmas party. Teggs felt very
content. His flight crew – fifty flying
reptiles called dimorphodon – were

hanging paper chains from the ceiling.
Arx, his triceratops deputy, was fiddling
with some fairy lights. And Iggy, the
ship's engineer, was getting messy
making a Christmas pudding.

"This will be the stickiest, slodgiest
pudding you ever tasted," the
iguanodon declared, stirring ferns into
the yellow mixture.

"It smells
delicious," said
Arx as the
warm glow of
the fairy lights
filled the
Sauropod. "But it
needs one special
ingredient . . ." He
produced some spiky leaves from
behind his back. "Holly!"

"That should certainly make it taste
sharper!" Iggy agreed.

Teggs chuckled. He loved Christmas.

He wondered what Papa Claws would bring him the day after tomorrow. Every year, the red-and-white-clad Santasaurus whizzed through space on a space-sleigh – delivering billions of presents to plant-eaters everywhere . . .

"Warning!" the alarm pterosaur squawked suddenly. "We're going to crash! SQUAAAAAWWWKKK!"

"*What?*" Iggy threw his pudding up into the air in shock, and it stuck to the ceiling.

"Quick, Iggy, slam on the brakes!" Teggs commanded, leaping into his control pit.

Iggy pulled on the big brake lever with all his strength. The *Sauropod* screeched to a halt.

Arx jumped into his chair and peered at his space radar. "The alarm pterosaur

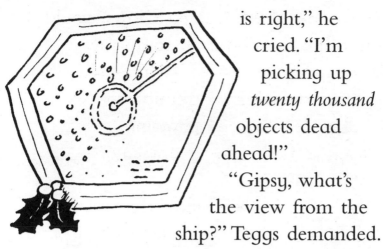

is right," he cried. "I'm picking up *twenty thousand* objects dead ahead!"

"Gipsy, what's the view from the ship?" Teggs demanded.

Gipsy's hoofs flicked over her controls, and the scanner screen glowed into life. Teggs stared out at the stars. They shone as white and bright as snowflakes. But some of those stars seemed to be getting bigger . . .

"Maybe they're meteors," said Iggy. "Lumps of space rock."

"Or perhaps they're little satellites," Gipsy wondered.

"I don't think they're satellites *or* space rocks," breathed Teggs. The shapes on the scanner were gleaming in the starlight as they drifted towards the ship. Some were

square, some were rectangular, some
were all knobbly and bobbly . . . and
they were all tied up with ribbons!

"They look like parcels!" Arx gasped
in astonishment. "I've heard of meteor
showers — but a shower of *gifts*, floating
in space . . . ?"

"Perhaps they fell off the back of a
spaceship," suggested Iggy.

Teggs had a horrible thought. "Or
maybe it's a trick," he said. "They
could be *booby-trapped* presents — left
here by CARNIVORES!"

Iggy's pudding fell from the ceiling and hit the floor with a wet splat, and the astrosaurs' festive moods went much the same way. Plant-eaters and meateaters shared the Jurassic Quadrant of space, but they didn't get on. Fights often broke out. It was the astrosaurs' job to keep the peace – and to keep the carnivores away!

"Wherever these presents came from, they are clogging up this part of space," said Arx. "That makes them a danger to passing ships."

"We must clear them away," Teggs decided.

"But we can't bring them on board until we know they aren't a danger to *us*," Iggy added. "Anything could be inside! Space bombs, killer slugs, acid mines . . ."

"You're right," Teggs declared, jumping out of his control pit. "I'll just have to take a space walk and check them out."

"*Cheep!*" said Sprite, the leader of the dimorphodon.

"All right, Sprite, you can come too," Teggs agreed. "Come on!"

The other astrosaurs shared worried looks as Teggs and Sprite left in the lift . . .

★

10

Five minutes later, dressed in protective armour and white, quilted spacesuits, Teggs and Sprite were floating out into space on the end of a safety rope.

Teggs felt a trickle of sweat run down the spiny plates on his back as he carefully caught one of the gifts. What if it *was* dangerous?

He read the label: "To Gladys Saurus, from Papa Claws." He blinked. "Papa Claws?"

The package looked innocent enough. But looks could be deceiving . . .

Slowly, Sprite undid the ribbon with his claws. Little by little the knot unravelled. Teggs held his breath as the dimorphodon gently pulled away the wrapping paper . . .

To reveal a pair of woolly bed socks!

"With this helmet on I can't smell them," Teggs said. "But they *look* harmless!"

Sprite nodded and flapped off to gather up more of the parcels.

Teggs frowned. "These are from Papa Claws too!" He tore them open. There were all sorts of things inside – scarves, hats, toy spaceships . . . *This is very strange*, he thought. *Very strange indeed.*

"Calling Gipsy," Teggs said into his communicator. "The presents seem to

be ordinary gifts – from Papa Claws.
Send out all the dimorphodon to
gather them up, double-quick."

"Yes, sir," said Gipsy. "But how come
presents from Papa Claws have been
dumped in the middle of space so close
to Christmas?"

"Either Papa Claws lost them," said
Arx, "or else something bad has
happened to him."

Teggs hauled himself back inside the
Sauropod. "Tell DSS HQ we can't make
their party tonight," he told Gipsy. "We
must return these presents to Papa
Claws and check he's OK – and fast!"

Chapter Two

JOURNEY TO EXMUS

There was no time to lose. While the dimorphodon flapped through space collecting up the presents, Teggs and Arx checked the top-secret star charts that showed the exact location of Papa Claws's space base.

"Papa Claws lives on Exmus," noted Arx. "It's an asteroid orbiting the North Pole Star."

"That's near the edge of the Jurassic Quadrant," Teggs realized, chewing on a juicy vine from the floor of his control pit. "We'll have to travel at top speed to get there in time."

As soon as the dimorphodon had scooped up every last gift and were safely aboard, the *Sauropod* headed for Exmus. The astrosaurs scraped up Iggy's extra-sticky Christmas pudding and ate it on the way. They even pulled some crackers. But no one felt very jolly.

At last, after many hours, an asteroid appeared on the scanner. It was shaped like an enormous candy cane. Green and red satellites glowed around it like Christmas lights.

"I think we've found the right place!" said Teggs. "Send a greetings message, Gipsy."

"Calling Exmus . . ." Gipsy spoke into her space microphone. "This is the DSS *Sauropod* . . ."

Suddenly, four glowing satellites whizzed towards them. They were round like Christmas baubles – with laser guns sticking out! "Halt!" came a robotic voice. "Identify yourselves or we will fire."

Teggs frowned. "And a merry Christmas to you too!"

"We are astrosaurs," said Gipsy quickly. "We come in peace."

Suddenly, the image of a small, stern dinosaur with pointy ears and an even pointier hat appeared on the scanner.

"That's an elfosaur," Arx observed. "Papa Claws employs them as helpers."

"I am Nickel, Head of Security," said the elfosaur. "Sorry about the rude welcome, astrosaurs. Some presents were stolen from Exmus last week – so now these security satellites defend us against any unknown ship."

"Well, you know us now," said Teggs. "And I think we might have *found* your stolen presents . . ."

Teggs explained all that had happened, and Nickel invited him to come down to Exmus in a shuttle. Arx, Gipsy and Iggy were allowed to come too. They took the presents in another four shuttles, which Iggy flew by remote control.

As they soared over the asteroid's snowy plains and mountains, Teggs felt a tingle of excitement. "Not many people are allowed to visit Exmus," he remarked. "Papa Claws is far too busy for visitors."

"I'd love to know how he delivers all those presents," said Arx. "He's the only Santasaurus in the universe, so he's very mysterious."

"And to think, we might get to meet him!" Gipsy grinned. "What a Christmas treat!"

Two doors opened up in the asteroid's frozen surface to reveal an underground parking bay covered in tinsel and streamers. It was full of space-sleighs

and empty carriages, waiting to be
loaded with goodies.

Iggy landed all
five shuttles with
his usual skill.
Then a
group of
elfosaurs dressed
in big red-and-
white furry
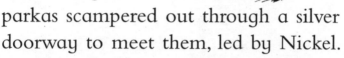
parkas scampered out through a silver
doorway to meet them, led by Nickel.

"Welcome to Exmus," said Nickel.
"May I check the presents, please?"

Iggy hit a button on his remote
control and the shuttle doors opened.
The elfosaurs rushed inside. In a blur of
movement they started sorting the
presents into neat piles.

Gipsy gasped. "They're so fast!"

Nickel nodded. "Papa sends out fifty
billion presents each year – so his
helpers *have* to be speedy!"

"These are the stolen presents, all right!" shouted a young elfosaur with one huge powerful arm and one that was skinny. "All twenty thousand of them. I recognize my handwriting."

Nickel saw the astrosaurs staring. "Writing fifty billion labels has given Hans mega-muscles!" he explained.

"But only in one arm!" Hans added.

"Well, thanks for returning these gifts," said Nickel. "But it's too late for us to use them now. Papa has had to buy replacements – if he hadn't, twenty thousand dinosaurs might have gone without presents!"

"What I don't understand is: who stole these gifts in the first place?" said Iggy.

"And how?" Gipsy added.

"And, more importantly, *why?*" said Arx.

"I don't know," Nickel confessed. "So far, I haven't found a single clue—"

Suddenly an alarm went off. "Ho-ho-NO!" it blared at top volume, "Ho-ho-*NOOOOO!*" The lights in the parking bay turned warning red, and the strands of tinsel hanging from the ceiling shook like rattlesnakes.

"What's happening?" Teggs demanded.

"That's the 'Whoops-naughty-no-you-don't' alarm!" cried Hans, putting his hands to his ears and almost squashing one side of his head. "Someone is opening presents before Christmas!"

Nickel checked a gadget on his shiny black belt. "It's coming from storehouse one . . ."

"Lead us there," said Teggs, taking charge. "Quick!"

Nickel sprinted away with a gaggle of elfosaurs. The astrosaurs followed them through a maze of wide, candy-striped corridors with sliding doors until they reached storehouse one. Its large metal door was standing ajar, and beyond it . . .

"Oh, no!" wailed Nickel, skidding to a sudden stop. Crossly, he hit a button on his belt. The alarm cut off and the lights went back to normal.

Teggs pushed past him and peered into the vast storeroom. It was the size of a supermarket and filled from floor to ceiling with a crumpled mess of torn wrapping paper, ripped ribbons and discarded gifts.

"Looks like we're too late," Teggs told his crew grimly. "The Christmas thieves have struck again. They're still here on Exmus!"

Chapter Three

INTRUDER ALERT!

"Whose presents were kept in here?" wondered Arx, nosing through the mess in the storeroom.

"That's the strange thing," said Nickel. "These are the very presents that Papa Claws bought to replace the ones that were stolen!"

"The first lot get stolen, the next lot get torn open," Gipsy mused. "Why?"

Teggs turned to Hans. "You wrote the labels. Is there anything special about the dinosaurs getting these presents?"

"Nope." Hans shook his head. "They're just ordinary folk from the Tri System."

"I'd better check what has been taken," said Nickel. He clicked his claws and the elfosaurs burst into action. Their bodies were a blur as they sorted through the wrecked wrapping paper and piled up the presents.

"*Nothing's* been taken!" Hans reported. "Whatever they were looking for, they didn't find it."

Nickel cheered up a bit. "The alarm must have scared them away."

"Perhaps . . ." said Arx, deep in thought.

"*Goodness me, whatever's going on here?*"
Teggs and his crewmates all jumped
at the sound of the high, twittery
voice. Then they gasped as an old, fat
dinosaur with a long white beard and
a big red hat came waddling round the
corner. His scaly skin was green, but
his cheeks were red. A pair of small,
round spectacles were perched on the
end of his snout.

"Papa Claws!" Gipsy gasped. "It's
really you!"

The newcomer smiled. "You must be one of those astrosaurs I heard arriving! What was that alarm about?"

"I'm afraid it was intruders again, sir," said Nickel. "They wrecked all those presents you bought!"

"But luckily we found the stolen presents dumped in deep space," Teggs explained. "I am Captain Teggs Stegosaur and this is my crew . . ." He introduced Arx, Gipsy and Iggy, and then smiled. "May I add, it's a real blast to meet you, sir. I've always wondered . . . what made you devote your whole life to Christmas like this?"

"Er . . ." Papa Claws shrugged. "I really wanted to play professional golf – but I wasn't good enough. So I took this up instead."

"I see," said Teggs, feeling a bit disappointed.

"Papa's only joking," said Nickel quickly. "Aren't you, Papa?"

The Santasaurus looked at him for a moment – then roared with laughter.

"Yes, of course I am!" he bellowed. "I'm here because I love Christmas. It's as simple as that!" Papa Claws started looking around. "Now, where are these intruders? I'll give them a piece of my mind!"

"I . . ." Nickel blushed. "I'm afraid they got away, sir."

"We will help Nickel find them," said Teggs. "Did you happen to see anything unusual on your way here?"

Papa Claws shook his head. "No, I'm afraid not."

"Then they must have gone the other way," Iggy realized, pointing down the corridor.

"There's an emergency exit that way," said Nickel. "It leads onto the surface. Let's go!"

"Iggy, come with me," said Teggs, running after Nickel. "Arx, Gipsy, you stay here and check for clues!"

Arx and Gipsy saluted.

"And perhaps you elfosaurs could tidy up this mess," said Papa Claws sadly.

"At once, Papa!" cried Hans, saluting with his big hand and almost knocking himself out.

"So many presents." The Santasaurus sighed. "Such a lot to do!"

"How do you manage to deliver so many billions of presents in a single night?" Arx wondered. "I mean – how do you get them all to the right addresses? How do you fit them in your space-sleighs?"

"Aha!" Papa Claws chuckled. "Trade secret. I use intelligent, self-propelled wrapping paper and a special short-term shrinking ray!"

Gipsy blinked. "*What?*"

"They're my own inventions," explained Papa Claws. "First, my elfosaurs wrap the presents and program each one with an address. Then my special ray shrinks the presents

31

down to the size of pinheads for easy loading and delivery."

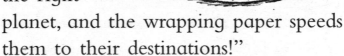

Arx gasped. "So all you have to do is drop the presents into orbit around the right planet, and the wrapping paper speeds them to their destinations!"

"Correct!" The Santasaurus beamed. "Once the gifts have delivered themselves down the chimneys, the shrinking ray wears off and they go back to normal size, ready for opening!"

"That's utterly brilliant!" Arx declared. "Can you give us a demonstration?"

Papa Claws smiled. "Perhaps, when I'm less busy," he said. "But right now I must be off to my workshop. Toodle-oo!"

With a wave, he waltzed away round the corner.

"What a shame." Arx sighed. "I'd love to see that shrinking ray in action!"

"Me too," said Gipsy — then noticed a piece of paper on the floor. "Hey,

look. Papa Claws dropped something."

Arx speared it with his horn. "It's a receipt! For twenty thousand presents bought

from the Rose Star Spaceport . . ." He frowned. "I've never heard of it."

"And I didn't know spaceports sold that many toys and gifts." Gipsy shrugged. "Oh, well. I'll go after him and give it back."

She clopped away down the candy-striped corridor after Papa

Claws, but he had already vanished from sight. Gipsy quickened her step, following the corridor's twists and turns.

Then, as she jogged round a sharp corner, she paused. There was a big silver door ahead of her, marked SHRINKING RAY CHAMBER. A complicated control panel sat just beside it.

"So *this* is where it all happens!" thought Gipsy. Overcome with curiosity, she opened the door and peeped inside.

Then she gasped –
as something hard
struck the back
of her head!
The world spun
around, and
Gipsy collapsed to
the floor . . .

Chapter Four

SURPRISE ATTACK

Outside on the surface of Exmus, Teggs, Iggy and Nickel were searching through the snow for any trace of the intruders.

"My tail's freezing off!" Iggy complained. "I hadn't realized how

c-c-c-cold it would be out here!"

Teggs was shivering too. "It's a waste of time looking out here anyway," he decided. "There's not a single track to be seen."

"I wish I knew what these intruders were after," said Nickel. "With all the amazing goodies we make here, why bother with the only gifts bought from somewhere else?"

Iggy nodded. "And why steal those presents we found dumped in space in the first place?"

Suddenly, Nickel gasped. "I just thought — I hope my super-special-secret Christmas surprise for Papa Claws is still safe!" In a panic, he charged off towards the parking bay and unlocked the door to a storeroom just inside the grotto's entrance. Teggs and Iggy tried to peek inside — but Nickel quickly shut the door and wiped his brow with relief. "Phew! The intruder hasn't touched it."

"What have you got Papa Claws, then?" Iggy asked.

Nickel went white with shock and almost fell over. "I can't tell you that before Christmas!" he spluttered.

"No one's allowed to look at their presents before Christmas, remember?"

Teggs reminded Iggy. "If he told you, he would probably set off an alarm!"

Suddenly they heard a distant cry from further inside the grotto: "*Help, someone! Quickly!*"

"Sounds like the alarm's gone off already," said Iggy grimly.

"And that's Arx's voice!" Teggs realized, bounding off through the corridors. "Come on!"

Following the sound of the cries, Teggs, Iggy and Nickel soon arrived at the Shrinking Ray Chamber. They found Arx, Hans and the other elfosaurs all gathered around a very groggy Gipsy. Hans tried to give her a

comforting pat on the back with his big hand, but nearly knocked her over.

Teggs gently curled his long tail around the stripy hadrosaur. "What happened, Gipsy?"

"I was looking for Papa Claws and passed the Shrinking Ray Chamber," she explained. "I tried to take a tiny peep – and was whacked on the back of the head!"

"Maybe someone was hiding behind the door," Iggy reasoned.

Teggs checked inside the large, metal room. "It's empty now."

Arx studied the control panel. "The shrinking ray has been used very recently – these controls are still warm."

"But there are no presents due for shrinking." Nickel frowned. "And that door is kept locked at all times!"

"The intruders must have opened it somehow," said Teggs. "No wonder we couldn't find their tracks outside – they're still somewhere in this base!"

"But what are they up to?" Arx frowned. "It doesn't make sense. First they steal some presents. Then they wreck the replacement presents but don't steal any. *Then* they start fiddling around with the shrinking ray . . ."

All of a sudden *another* alarm went off!

Arx groaned. "I can't keep up with them!"

"Jingle-jingle-STOP!" went the alarm. "Jingle-jingle-STOP!"

41

"That's the auto-sorting packing area alarm," cried Nickel, checking the gadget on his belt. "Yes, look – conveyor-belt six has been stopped."

Hans was baffled. "But why would the intruders want to stop presents being wrapped?"

"We'll ask them when we catch them!" shouted Teggs. "Quickly, Nickel, take us to conveyor-belt six – they won't get away from us again!"

Once again, Teggs sprinted off through the stripy corridors. But this time he ordered Iggy, Gipsy and Arx to stand guard with some of the elfosaurs at key points along the way.

"I've got an astrosaur standing at every exit from the packaging block," he explained to Nickel and Hans as they ran. "The intruders won't be able to get past us this time!"

"Nice one!" said Hans. He slapped

Teggs heartily on the back and almost flattened him.

As they turned the next corner, Nickel stopped running and turned off the alarm. He pointed to a large, orange door. "This is the place."

"Any elfosaurs working in there?" asked Teggs.

"Only some wrapping robots," Nickel told him. "Everything is automatic."

"OK, I'll go in first," said Teggs. "Get ready to follow me." He took a deep breath, reared up – and smashed down the door!

Swishing his spiky tail about, Teggs burst into the huge warehouse and quickly took in the scene. Everything was silent and still. The large conveyor belt in the middle of the room had been switched off. Big, blocky wrapping robots stood beside the belt like towering statues, holding sheets of sparkling paper in their metal mitts. Above them, mechanical scoops dangled lifelessly from the ceiling on super-tough tinsel.

"Spread out," Teggs hissed.

The three dinosaurs went in different directions. Teggs sorted quickly through the pile of wrapped presents at the far end of the conveyor belt – but there was no one hiding there. Nickel  looked behind some crates and Hans checked that the hatch in the ceiling was secure.

Teggs scratched his head. "There's no one here!"

Nickel pointed to a glowing red light above a big switch on one wall. "But someone has hit the emergency stop!"

Teggs spoke into his wrist communicator. "Arx, Gipsy, Iggy, has anyone tried to get past you?"

"No," said all three of his friends at once.

Teggs looked grimly at Hans and Nickel. "Then whoever hit the emergency stop and set off the alarms *must* still be here!"

Suddenly, there was a loud mechanical hiss behind them – and one of the wrapping robots lurched into life! Its eyes glowed eerie yellow and a wisp of steam curled from its jagged mouth. It threw away its paper. Its fingers curled into fists . . . And then the robot hurled itself at Captain Teggs!

Chapter Five

THE METAL MENACE

Teggs barely managed to duck out of
the way as the wrapping robot lunged
for his throat. "Is that normal
behaviour for this thing?" he gasped.

"No!" cried Nickel, as the robot knocked him aside. "It's gone haywire!"

Hans raised his big muscly arm and tried to tackle the robot – but in a blur of movement the robot whacked him on the head! With a groan, the elfosaur fell to the ground.

"Crew!" Teggs snapped into his communicator. "I need your help – FAST!"

The robot grabbed Nickel and raised him up above its head. But Teggs socked the tin terror with his tail – *CLANG!* It staggered back, and Nickel was able to wriggle free.

"Get Hans out of the way!" Teggs shouted. "I'll distract this ridiculous robo-wrapper . . ."

Nickel hurried to obey, as the robot rushed towards Teggs. It grabbed hold of his tail and twisted hard, its hands moving with power and precision.

"Ow!" Teggs yelled. "It's trying to fold me up!"

Suddenly, Iggy, Arx and Gipsy came running into the room. Arx lowered his head and charged the

robot, bashing it away from Teggs.
Gipsy gave it a hoof-jab and a tail-
swipe, knocking it to its knees. Then
Iggy zapped it with his stun claws. The
wrapping robot steamed and hissed,
then fell over backwards and lay still.

"Thanks, guys," said Teggs, beaming
round at his crew. "That seems to be
one metal menace all *wrapped up!*"

Suddenly, Papa Claws appeared in
the doorway blinking in surprise. "I
heard the alarm. What's going on?" He

frowned. "And what's Hans doing, lying down on the job? It's almost Christmas Eve!"

"He's not lying down," said Nickel grimly. "He was *pushed* down – by that robot!"

"Bless my tinsel!" Papa Claws exclaimed.

"Is Hans OK?" asked Gipsy.

Nickel nodded as Hans groaned noisily. "He'll be fine. He's just got a nasty bump on his head."

"We should start a club!" Gipsy joked.

"Well, at least we've finally found the 'intruder' round here," said Teggs. "A wrapping robot that's gone wrong!"

Nickel sighed. "In all my years here on Exmus, I've never known one go crazy like that before."

"Perhaps it was trying to *re-wrap* those presents in storehouse one," Iggy suggested.

"Of course!" Papa Claws declared. "And I remember now – a wrapping robot passed me in the corridor just before I met you there. I thought nothing of it at the time . . ."

"I suppose it must have whapped me on the head when I came looking for you, Papa Claws," said Gipsy. "That reminds me . . ." She pulled a bit of paper from her pocket. "You dropped this receipt for those gifts you bought at the Rose Star Spaceport . . ."

"Did I?" Papa Claws peered at the paper and chuckled. "Ah, yes, I have dealt with these people many times. They have an excellent gift shop there . . ." He passed it to Nickel. "Here you are — for those files of yours."

"Thank you, sir," said Nickel happily. "As you know, I like to keep track of everyone you deal with, for security reasons."

"Where *is* the Rose Star Spaceport, sir?" Arx asked him.

"Never mind that!" cried Teggs, prodding the fallen wrapping robot

with his tail. "What *I* want to know is how our robot friend sent twenty thousand presents into deep space in the first place – and what else it might have been up to!"

"Good question!" said Papa Claws.

"Iggy's good with robots," Gipsy pointed out. "Can you fix it up and make it talk, Ig?"

"Maybe," said Iggy. "I'll fetch my toolkit from the shuttle and give it a go."

He jogged from the room. Suddenly, a clock on the wall chimed. Teggs looked up and found it was midnight.

"It's Christmas Eve!" Papa Claws declared. "Goodness me, and there's still so much to do! I must get busy in my private workshop. But first . . ." He hurried over to the emergency stop switch and flicked it back on. The big conveyor belt clanked into life, the ceiling scoops dropped presents onto it, and the remaining robot started wrapping.

"Oh dear," said Nickel. "With only one robot left, it'll take twice as long to wrap the presents. And that means Papa will be late with his Christmas deliveries!"

"We could help with the wrapping," Teggs offered. Arx and Gipsy nodded keenly.

Papa Claws looked hopeful. "Really?"

"And I'll help too," said Nickel firmly. "Now we have caught our so-called 'intruder', there's nothing else for me to do tonight!"

"Thank you, all of you!" cried Papa Claws. "But first, Nickel, you must take Hans back to his room for a rest. Then prepare our guest rooms for Captain Teggs and his crew so they can get some sleep later."

Nickel smiled. "I'll get straight onto it."

"Thanks, Papa Claws," said Teggs, crossing to the conveyor belt. "And, er . . . any chance of a midnight feast?" He grinned as his stomach made some very rude noises. "Fighting robots always leaves me hungry!"

★

Within twenty minutes Iggy had fetched his toolkit, Nickel had tucked up Hans in bed, and Teggs had eaten three small Christmas trees. Now he helped Nickel, Arx and Gipsy wrap presents while Iggy took the back off the robot's head and started poking around.

As the hours passed, Iggy ran test after test. But he couldn't find anything wrong with the robot's brain.

Gipsy yawned. Her hoofs were aching from so much wrapping. "How many more presents to go, Nickel?"

Nickel taped down a flap of paper. "This was the last one for this batch," he said. "Well done, everyone. Now we can take a break."

"Good!" Arx stretched. "It's been a long day."

"Let's grab some sleep," Teggs suggested.

Nickel showed them to their rooms, which were side by side in one of the stripy corridors. Iggy had brought the wrapping robot's head and his toolkit with him.

"Most people prefer a teddy bear," said Teggs cheekily.

"I'm determined to find out what went wrong with this thing," Iggy replied. "I won't be able to sleep until I do!"

The astrosaurs said goodnight to each other and went to their rooms.

Iggy found a present waiting for him on his bed. He read the label: *Happy Christmas! Thanks a lot, from Papa Claws.* "Well, it's *nearly* Christmas," said Iggy. "I'm sure I won't set off any alarms if I open it now."

He quickly tore open the paper. "Oh! A green tie." Iggy was a bit disappointed. He didn't wear ties. "Still, it's the thought that counts . . ."

Putting the tie to one side, he started rummaging once more through the robot's wires and circuits.

But then he heard a scraping sound behind him.

Iggy turned – and gasped. With its fangs gleaming and claws outstretched, a ravenous *raptor* was standing right behind him!

Chapter Six

A FRIGHT IN THE NIGHT

Before Iggy could even open his mouth to yell, the raptor attacked. Desperately, he grabbed the savage carnivore's scaly orange wrists, struggling to keep its claws out of his face.

"*Ssstupid asssstrosaur,*" the raptor hissed angrily. "You should have kept your nose out of our business. Now I musssst bite it off!"

"You can try, ugly!" growled Iggy. He suddenly did a backward roll and flipped the raptor over his head. It crashed into the wall. "Where did you spring from?"

But the raptor's only reply was to

jump up, ready to attack again.

As it charged towards him, Iggy grabbed his new tie and cracked it out like a whip. The green fabric whipped around the raptor's ankle, and Iggy yanked on it hard. With a squeak of surprise, the raptor was jerked off his feet and crashed against the head of the wrapping robot. It collapsed, knocked senseless.

Suddenly, Iggy's door was thrown
open and Teggs burst inside. Arx and
Gipsy were just behind him. "Are you
all right, Ig?" Teggs cried. "We heard—
Good grief!"

"A velociraptor!" gasped Gipsy.

Teggs noticed the torn wrapping
paper. "Don't tell me Papa Claws gave
you a raptor for Christmas?"

"It came out of nowhere," said Iggy.
"Papa Claws gave me a tie – and
without it, I would have ended up as
sliced iguanodon!"

"Hey, look here," said Arx, frowning.

The raptor had
knocked open
a cover inside
the robot's
head,
revealing a
bundle of
wires sliced in
two. "Someone has cut
through its brain-cords. This robot was
made to go wrong."

"You're right!" Iggy groaned. "I spent
all that time checking the robot's
programming, but I didn't think to
check for sabotage."

Teggs took a look. "Hey, what's that
thing stuck in the robot's braincase?"

Gipsy pulled out a small, sharp,
ivory curl. "It looks like . . . part of a
claw!"

"Then the raptor definitely did this,"
said Teggs slowly. "It tricked us into
blaming a robot for these weird

goings-on – putting us off the scent to buy itself time!"

"*This* raptor didn't do it," said Gipsy. "All its claws are intact."

Iggy shuddered. "They were almost in *me!*"

"Obviously, there is more than one raptor on Exmus," Arx observed.

"And whatever they're up to, we've got to stop them," said Teggs. "Arx, Iggy, go and fetch Nickel. We must start a full-scale search of the whole grotto."

"Yes, sir," said Arx. "At least we know what we're looking for this time!"

Teggs nodded. "And, Gipsy, you and I must find Papa Claws and warn him. Rudolph the Red-nosed *Raptor* here is solid proof – carnivores have come to spoil Christmas!"

Teggs and Gipsy carried the sleeping raptor between them as they rushed along the red-and-white striped corridors, following signs for Papa Claws's private workshop. At last they found it, at the most northerly point of the grotto. Fairy lights winked and twinkled all around the frosted windows, and statues of candy canes and snowsaurs stood either side of the big bronze entrance.

"What if Papa Claws is asleep?" whispered Gipsy. "After all, he's got a long day ahead of him tomorrow."

"Let's find out," said Teggs. He knocked on the door. There was no reply. So he tried the door handle — but that wouldn't budge. "The door's locked," he remarked.

"Perhaps he's popped out."

Gipsy looked at him. "Or maybe that's what the raptors *want* us to think! Papa Claws said he was coming here. What if the raptors are holding him prisoner?"

"You're right, Gipsy. We had better find out," Teggs muttered.

Together, Teggs and Gipsy kicked open the door, rushed inside and jumped into battle poses.

But the workshop was quiet and empty. There was no sign that Papa Claws had been working on anything at all.

"I don't understand," said Teggs. "Papa Claws said he had so much to do—"

"Shh!" said Gipsy. "Listen!"

Loud, scuffling footsteps were drawing closer to the workshop.

"Quick!" said Teggs. "Hide behind this workbench . . ."

He and Gipsy ducked out of sight
with their sleeping prisoner, just as
Papa Claws came in – flanked by five
nasty-looking green raptors!

"The gifts from conveyor-belt six
have been shrunk and loaded onto
your space-sleigh," said the tallest
raptor. "All is now prepared . . ."

"What can we do?" hissed Gipsy.
"We must save Papa Claws!"

But Teggs's jaw had dropped open. "Wait," he whispered, peeping round the side of the bench. "*Look at his hand!*"

Gipsy looked, and gasped. One of the claws on Papa's left hand was broken! She thought back to the piece of claw she had found in the wrapping robot's head . . .

"Where has that useless Ranpak got to?" Papa Claws complained, offering the raptors a seat. "All I asked him to do was to squish that stupid iguanodon before he found out I sabotaged that wrapping robot . . . What's keeping him?"

"The raptors have turned Papa Claws space-crazy!" said Teggs. "They've made him as nasty as they are!"

Gipsy gulped and nodded. "In more ways than one. Look!"

The astrosaurs stared in horror as Papa Claws put his hands to his beard and pulled. His scaly face stretched like rubber – then pinged off! Underneath his disguise, "Papa Claws" looked very different – he was a large, horrid-looking raptor! His whole head was scuffed and scraped. One eye was hidden by a black patch, but the other gleamed with sly cunning.

"It can't be . . ." croaked Gipsy.

"But it is!" Teggs gulped. "It's our oldest enemy, the rottenest raptor of the lot – *General Loki!*"

Chapter Seven

THE PLAN OF EVIL

"That's better!" snarled General Loki, scratching his ugly face. "How I hate pretending to be Papa Claws. Having to act sweet and nice and kind all day – it makes me sick!"

"But it is worth it," said one of the raptors.

"Thanks to your brilliant plan, General, we shall sssoon take over the entire Vegetarian Sssector!"

"Not if the astrosaurs can help it!" cried Teggs, leaping out from hiding.

"And we *can!*" added Gipsy. She jumped through the air and took out two raptors with a well-placed tail-swipe.

Loki snarled with surprise and tried to bite Gipsy. Teggs shoulder-charged

him and knocked him reeling across the workshop. The other three raptors dived at Teggs, their jaws snapping. But Teggs twirled his tail around so fast he actually took off into the air! Unable to stop, the raptors knocked into each other and collapsed in a heap on the floor – so Teggs stopped spinning his tail and landed with a *SPLAT* on top of all three.

"That about wraps it up for you raptors," Teggs snarled.

"Are you ssso ssssure?" rasped another
raptor – the one they had left behind
the desk. Now it had woken up and
had Gipsy in a hooflock!"Ssssurrender,"
it hissed. "Or I will turn your friend
into hadrosaur hamburgers!"

"Sorry, Captain!" exclaimed Gipsy.
"He crept up behind me."

"Sneaky work, Ranpak," said General
Loki approvingly. "And to make doubly

sure, Teggs – if you give me any
trouble, I shall give *my* prisoner a claw
sandwich!"

Teggs climbed off the dazed raptors
and whirled round – to find Loki was
now holding the *real* Papa Claws at
tooth-point.

"Papa
Claws!" Teggs
gasped. "Are
you all right?"

"No!" The
Santasaurus
looked
bewildered
and cross.
"This
brute
has had
me locked up
in a cupboard here for days! Asking me
this, asking me that, making me teach
him everyone's names . . ."

Teggs scowled at Loki. "So no one here would suspect you weren't the real Papa."

"I even used a voice changer to sound exactly like your sappy Santasaurus!" Loki agreed. "A perfect impersonation!"

Loki's raptor bodyguards got back up and surrounded Teggs, clicking their claws threateningly. But Teggs ignored them. "How did you even get here, Loki?" he demanded. "Last I heard, you were in a maximum-security space prison."

"I escaped!" cried Loki.

"Do you seriously think there is a jail in the universe that can hold me? Me, Commander of the Seven Fleets of Death? Ruler of the meat mines of Raptos? Tamer of T. rex, destroyer of diplodocus—?"

"And the biggest dino-*bore* in space," Teggs interrupted, yawning noisily. But for all his joking, he was secretly very worried. Twice before he had tangled with Loki — once at the Great Dinosaur Games, and once on the eerie planet Creepus — and both times, he had barely survived. "I suppose you're planning to spoil Christmas for everyone and then conquer the entire Vegetarian Sector," he went on. "You are so predictable, Loki."

Loki frowned. "I am not!"

"I just *knew* you were going to say that," said Teggs.

"Your pathetic jokes don't fool me, Captain," said Loki. "You're dying to know what I've been up to, aren't you? I bet you'd love to find out the juicy details of my entire plan!"

"Go on then," said Teggs. "I like a good bedtime story."

"When you hear this, you will never sleep again!" Loki hissed. "First, I landed on the surface of Exmus in a ship disguised as a lump of space junk. There was room inside for just seven of us, all squashed up together."

Gipsy turned up her nose. "What a stinky ship *that* must have been!"

Loki ignored her and tightened his grip on Papa Claws. "My raptors sneaked inside and stole twenty thousand presents. They loaded them on a space-sleigh and dumped them out in deep space . . ."

"Where we found them," Teggs realized. "And while your raptors were away, you snuck in, locked up Papa Claws and took his place, right?"

Loki nodded. "And the first thing I did as 'Papa Claws' was order replacements for the missing presents – from my home planet, Raptos!"

"But we saw the receipt," said Gipsy. "You bought them from the Rose Star Spaceport."

"Ha! Astro-fool! That was my little joke – there's no such place. But I *had* to forge a receipt to keep that numbskull Nickel happy."

"Of course," groaned Papa Claws. "If you scramble up the letters in Rose

Star Spaceport you get RAPTOR
SPACE STORES!"

Teggs blinked. "However did you
work that out?"

Papa Claws shrugged. "I spend eight
months of the year in bed recovering
after Christmas," he said. "I get through
a lot of cryptic crosswords."

Gipsy smiled. "You are very clever!"

"Shut up!" snarled Loki furiously.
"*I'm* the clever one, not him! I built
perfect replicas of plant-eater cargo
ships to fool the security satellites into
letting them land. Like Nickel, they
thought the ships were bringing

replacement presents — but those ships were *also* bringing in an army of twenty thousand raptor troops!"

Gipsy gasped. "Where did you hide so many raptors?"

"They were camping out on the surface of Exmus," Papa Claws piped up. "Waiting until Loki was ready for the practice-run of his miserable master plan."

Loki's good eye glinted in the light. "First, I used Papa Claws's shrinking ray to reduce my raptors to a tiny size. Then I hid each of them inside a present. At my signal, each of the raptors returned to normal size—"

"And so they burst out of the wrapping paper!" Gipsy realized.

Teggs nodded. "That explains all the mess we found in storeroom one, and why our so-called 'intruder' didn't take anything."

"That's right." Loki smiled nastily. "Then, in my Papa Claws disguise, I took my troops straight back to the Shrinking Ray Chamber. When you asked me later if I'd seen anything unusual, I almost laughed my beard off!"

"So it was *you* who hit me on the head before I could look inside the Shrinking Ray Chamber," Gipsy said. "You had to stop me from finding them!"

"Whacking you was a real pleasure," Loki told her.

"So now we know . . ." Teggs glared at Loki. "You're planning to shrink down your raptors and package them up with Christmas gifts, ready to be delivered all around the Vegetarian Sector!"

"There will be widespread panic and chaos," Loki agreed. "And while it rages on, I shall lead my fleets of death in a glorious invasion . . ." The general threw back his head and laughed, and Ranpak and his raptor mates all joined in. "This is going to be a Christmas that no one will ever forget!"

Chapter Eight

DOWN THE CHUTE!

As Loki laughed on, Teggs looked helplessly between Gipsy and Papa Claws, both stuck tight in the grip of the raptors. He had to do something –

but what? Even if he managed to save one of them, the other would surely be squished.

"And now, my dear Captain, it is time I dealt with you and your friends once and for all," snarled General Loki, snapping his jaws. "I know it's only Christmas Eve – but I fancy a bit of Christmas dinner . . ."

Then, suddenly, the workshop window smashed into a million pieces – as Iggy burst through it!

"If you're hungry, Loki, chew on this!" the iguanodon roared, socking the general in the jaw. Loki let go of Papa Claws as he was sent staggering backwards.

It was all the distraction Gipsy needed. She elbowed Ranpak in the stomach and stamped on his foot. Then she ducked down as Teggs swung his spiky tail and knocked the raptor flying. The other five raptors hissed and screeched and advanced on Teggs . . .

But a moment later, Arx burst inside, bellowing a battle cry as he charged. He squashed two raptors into the floor before butting Loki in the bottom. The general yelled in anger as he went crashing into the wall.

That left Teggs facing three angry raptors. "Since it's Christmas, I'll give you some mistletoe," he said. "Or do I mean – MISSILE-TOE?!" With that, he kicked one of the raptors so hard its head went through the ceiling!

The other two raptors pounced towards him. Gipsy grabbed one and hurled it over to Arx and Iggy, who whacked it with their tails at the same time. Then Nickel and Hans rushed into the workshop and dealt with the last raptor standing. Hans swatted it senseless with his big hand, and Nickel nutted it. It fell with a crash into the workbench.

"We did it!" cried Gipsy.

"Well done, all of you!" said Papa Claws, mopping his scaly brow. "Phew!"

"Hans, tie up these raptors," said Nickel, helping Papa Claws sit down in a chair. "Looks like you'll have to make an extra Christmas delivery tomorrow – to the nearest space prison!"

Teggs grinned as Hans started tying the raptors' claws together with extra-strong tinsel, then turned to Arx. "Did you hear Loki's plan?"

"Most of it, Captain," said Arx. "We were right outside, waiting for the best moment to burst in."

"But why did you follow us here?"

Gipsy wondered. "I thought you were searching the base."

"Well, I was still bothered by the fact I had never heard of the Rose Star Spaceport," said Arx eagerly, "even though 'Papa Claws' said he had used it many times before. Then I realized that if you unscramble the letters you get—"

"Raptor Space Stores?" asked Teggs brightly.

"Oh." Arx's horns crumpled. "You already know."

"Well done for working it out, my boy," said the real Papa Claws kindly.

"Once clever-clogs Arx worked that out, we thought something funny must be going on," Iggy added, tying up Ranpak with some fallen fairy lights. "And it certainly explains where that raptor in my room came from – he zoomed up to full size when I opened my present."

"Right!" snarled General Loki from the back of the workshop. Unnoticed by all, he had sneaked over to a hatch

in the wall and pulled it open. "And tomorrow, the same thing will happen on a thousand worlds! You may have beaten a handful of raptors – but you will never stop twenty thousand!"

Teggs frowned. "You're bluffing, Loki."

But Loki shook his head. "When I stopped conveyor-belt six, I didn't just sabotage the wrapping robot – I hid my troops inside the presents there!"

"Conveyor-belt six?" gasped Papa Claws. "But that handles gifts for the most important dinosaurs on every plant-eating planet!"

"Oh, no!" Gipsy groaned. "We even helped to wrap up those presents!"

"Ha, ha, ha!" Loki cackled. "Tomorrow morning, the Vegetarian Sector's leaders will be breakfast for my ravenous raptor army!"

"Get him!" Teggs cried.

But Loki had already wriggled away down the hatch.

"Papa Claws, where does that lead?" asked Arx.

"It's my private-jet chute — a short cut to the parking bay," the Santasaurus explained. "I simply jump in there and slide down straight into the pilot's seat of my space-sleigh."

Gipsy's head-crest flushed blue with alarm. "But Loki's raptor parcels have been shrunk and loaded onto that sleigh. He's all set to put his plan into action!"

"Quick, crew," cried Teggs. "We can't let Loki get away!"

He squeezed inside the chute and went whizzing down a slippery metal slide, faster and faster, like something out of a funfair. Then he shot out into the parking bay and skidded along the ground on his bottom.

Iggy popped out a moment later and landed on Teggs's back with a gasp – just before Gipsy and Arx flew out of the chute and fell on them both – "*OOF!*"

"Loki's getting away," groaned Teggs, struggling to his feet. "Look!"

The roof doors of the parking bay had slid open, ready for launch. The astrosaurs gazed up at the snowy mountains all around, at the endless starry night, at the red-and-green glow of the security satellites – and at the sleek space-sleigh rising up into space, towing a massive carriage filled with deadly presents behind it.

Loki's voice echoed out over the space-sleigh's loudspeakers as he steered close to a mountain. "Before I go," he called, "I've got one final Christmas

present that will stop you coming after
me . . ."

"We'll *never* stop coming after you!"
shouted Teggs.

But suddenly, fierce flames shot out
from the sleigh's rocket jets and
engulfed the top of the mountain. The
astrosaurs felt the ground shake – as an
avalanche of snow came roaring down
the mountainside, heading their way!

"Loki's trying to bury us beneath
tons of snow," yelled Arx. "We'll all be
squashed!"

"We have to get those roof doors closed!" cried Teggs.

"It's no good," said Iggy, who had already run to the controls. "Loki has smashed them – those doors are jammed open!"

The ground was shaking more and more. Gipsy shrieked, as the giant, jagged wave of snow and sleet came crashing down towards them . . .

Chapter Nine

DANGER AT THE EDGE OF SPACE

"Quick! Back inside the grotto!" Teggs ordered, and the astrosaurs ran for their lives. Already the first icy rocks and pebbles were pouring between the roof doors . . .

They jumped through the main entrance and slammed the doors behind them — just as half the mountainside came down on the parking bay, burying all the other space-sleighs along with the *Sauropod*'s shuttles.

"Loki's right," groaned Iggy. "We *can't* go after him now. He's beaten us!"

Just then, Nickel and Hans came running down the corridor with dozens of angry elfosaurs.

"We've told everyone what's been going on, and we all want to help you stop Loki," said Nickel.

"Yeah!" cried Hans. "What are we waiting for?"

"Spring, by the looks of it!" said Iggy sadly. He opened the doors to reveal  solid snow and ice from floor to ceiling. "An early thaw is about our only chance!"

"Well, I'm a *thaw* loser," Teggs declared. "We can't give up. There *must* be a way to stop Loki."

"We could send a message into space," Gipsy suggested. "Warning people not to open any presents tomorrow."

"I had the same idea," said Papa Claws, padding sadly towards them. "I went to the signals room to send a distress call — but Loki has smashed all the radios."

"I'll try my communicator and warn the *Sauropod*," said Teggs. But he got nothing but static. "All that ice on top of us must be blocking the signal!"

"Looks like Loki's thought of everything," said Iggy.

"Not quite," said Nickel. He turned to Papa Claws. "I'm sorry about this, sir, but . . . I'm going to have to ask you to open a present before Christmas Day."

Papa Claws was so shocked, his beard stood up in the air. "How can you suggest such a thing, Nickel?" he spluttered.

"Because us elfosaurs have all chipped in to buy you a brand-new Mega-Turbo Dungstar Five space-sleigh for Christmas, that's why!" Nickel unlocked a door in the wall to reveal a sleek, glittering, red-and-silver dream machine.

"So that's the super-secret surprise present you were on about, Nickel!" said Iggy, almost foaming at the mouth as he checked it out. "It's the super-swish sports car of space-sleighs." He sniffed the dung-tanks at the back. "Better yet, she's all fuelled up and ready to go!"

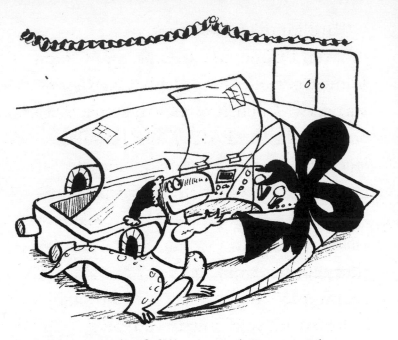

"It's wonderful!" gasped Papa Claws. "I don't know what to say!"

"How about, 'Please borrow it, astrosaurs, and chase after Loki before it's too late'?" Nickel suggested.

Gipsy frowned. "But what good is a space-sleigh down here? We can't drive it through solid snow and ice!"

"True," Nickel agreed. "But we *could* use its jet rockets as a blowtorch to melt our way out!"

"Brilliant!" cried Teggs.

"Stand aside, my friends," said Papa Claws, getting aboard his Christmas surprise. "When it comes to space-sleighs, I truly am the PAPA!" He skilfully steered the space-sleigh out of the storeroom and backed up towards the open doors. "Here goes!" he yelled, and hit a big yellow button. Super-hot blue flames burst from the jets and started melting the ice.

"It's working!" Gipsy squealed.

"Biggest blowtorch in the universe," said Teggs with a grin.

Hans flexed his big, strong arm. "Let's get using it, then!"

With Hans's help, the astrosaurs hoisted the sleigh onto their shoulders and used its powerful jets to melt a large tunnel through the ice. Steam choked them, and boiling ice-water

splashed and stung their skin. But at last they broke through the final frozen barriers and set down the sleigh on the asteroid's icy surface.

"We did it!" Gipsy cheered, kissing Hans on the cheek. The elfosaur blushed, put his hand to his face — and accidentally slapped himself unconscious.

"Good work, guys," said Teggs, helping Papa Claws out of the space-sleigh. "Now, come on, Iggy. We're going to stop Loki if it's the last thing we do."

"I hope it isn't!" said Iggy nervously.

"And meanwhile, everyone else must help to clear away this snow and ice," Teggs went on. "It's Christmas tomorrow."

"Well, squash my satsuma — you're right!" Papa Claws realized. "And every sleigh is still buried down there. I won't be able to make a single delivery until the parking bay is cleared!"

"Now we're on the surface I can call the *Sauropod* down from orbit," said Arx. "The ship's lasers will help us melt away the ice."

"Good luck, Arx," said Teggs, as Iggy climbed into the pilot seat beside him and revved the engines. "Now, take us up, Iggy. The lives of millions are at

stake – and so is Christmas itself!"

With a roar of power, the space-sleigh sped into the glittering darkness of the skies above.

The chase was on!

"Top speed, Iggy!" Teggs commanded as the space-sleigh shot away from Exmus. "Come on, put your foot down!"

"Sorry, Captain," said Iggy, flicking some switches on the dashboard. "Just working out what everything does . . ."

"There's no time for that now!" cried Teggs.

Iggy smiled to himself. "I think some of these controls *might* come in useful . . ."

On they roared through deepest space. They flew for hours, through stars scattered thick against the darkness like a storm of snowflakes. It was a beautiful sight. But nothing could distract Teggs from searching out the shining shape of General Loki's stolen space-sleigh.

"Look, there!" Teggs yelled, pointing to a shiny orange speck up ahead. "That must be him!"

"Are you sure?" said Iggy.

Then the orange speck suddenly turned and sped towards them – and opened fire with bright-green laser beams!

"I'm sure, all right," yelled Teggs. "Dodge those lasers, Iggy!"

"On the case, Captain," said Iggy, yanking down on the space-sleigh's joystick. He sent them spinning in a spiral, barely missing the blasts of deadly green light that went whizzing past the windows.

"I didn't think that Loki would be armed," said Teggs. "But it looks like he means to *sleigh* us!"

"Loki must have built secret lasers into that thing in case of trouble," Iggy reasoned. "Typical nasty raptor thinking."

Teggs spotted a space rock close by. "Quick, hide behind that meteor!"

Iggy steered in a big circle – but before he could reach the meteor, Loki blew it up!

"We'll have to keep running," said Teggs, as laser fire raked through the darkness either side of them. "Luckily, Loki is a rotten shot!"

"I don't think he's trying to hit us,"
said Iggy. "He's *herding* us. Those laser
blasts are forcing us to fly in a straight
line . . ."

Teggs checked the star maps. "We're
heading for the Vegmeat Zone," he
realized. "The no-man's land between
plant-eaters and meat-eaters . . ."

"And look!" Iggy gasped, pointing
through the windscreen. "It's full of
raptor death ships!"

Teggs saw the carnivore crafts
hanging in space ahead of them like a
row of giant, pointed teeth. "That must

be Loki's invasion fleet," he said quietly. "I have never seen so many death ships before."

"Calling Captain Teggs," came a nasty hiss from the space-sleigh's speakers. "I'm afraid your luck has finally run out. I am driving you into range of my death ships' weapons — and if you try to turn back, I will blast you to bits myself!"

The death ships were getting closer, shining like blood-red icicles in the starlight. Teggs and Iggy were on a collision course!

Chapter Ten

A FESTIVE FATE

"Sorry, Ig," said Teggs quietly. "Looks like this is one Christmas we won't be celebrating. I was in such a hurry to catch Loki, I didn't stop to think we weren't carrying a single weapon."

"Don't worry, Captain," said Iggy, frantically pressing buttons on the dashboard. "Loki and his fleet have a surprise coming. We may not be carrying a single weapon . . . but we *have* brought some along with us!"

"Eh?" Teggs stared at him. "What do you mean?"

"These top-of-the-range space-sleighs use super-magnets to tow carriages

behind them."
Iggy grinned
and patted the
dashboard.
"And before
we left
Exmus, I
boosted our
magnetic
power . . ."

Suddenly, something sparkled in the
corner of Teggs's eye. He turned to
the back window – and frowned. Four
glowing red-and-green baubles were
whizzing along just behind General
Loki's sleigh . . .

"Wait a minute!" spluttered Teggs.
"Those things look like the security
satellites orbiting Exmus!"

"That's because they ARE!" cried
Iggy. "I've been towing them along
with super-magnet power ever since
we left!"

Teggs felt excitement building in his belly. "And if I remember rightly, they are programmed to defend themselves against any unknown ship . . ."

Iggy grinned. "So let's see how they get on with a whole fleet of them!"

With a flick of his claws, Iggy sent a magnetic power-surge through the security satellites. The giant baubles went shooting on ahead of them like missiles . . .

"Halt!" grated the security satellites as they zoomed up to the death ships. "Identify yourselves, or we will fire!"

Caught by surprise, the crews of the death ships did not reply — and so the satellites let loose their laser bolts!

"Yee-hah!" cried Iggy, as the skies ahead of them were lit up with red-and-green laser fire.

"Return fire, you fools!" raged Loki over the speakers. "Destroy those oversized Christmas decorations! Destroy those *astrosaurs*!"

But, caught off-guard by the nippy satellites and firing wildly in all directions, the raptor ships only succeeded in destroying each other.

Fierce explosions dazzled Teggs and Iggy as one of the giant war-craft was blown apart. Another soon followed.

"Get us out of here, Iggy!" Teggs commanded.

They turned away from the exploding fleet, back towards Exmus – but General Loki was still on their tail, close behind.

"Astrosaur scum!" Loki's voice was a high-pitched squeal as he really let rip with his lasers. "I'll get you!"

Iggy was gripping the joystick for dear life. "We can't dodge this gunfire for much longer, Captain!"

"You'll pay!" Loki screeched, drawing nearer and nearer. "You'll pay for ruining my Christmas!"

"Sorry, Loki," said Teggs grimly, as laser beams zipped past, millimetres from his window, "but I think it's time that *you* paid for ruining ours. And the buck stops – HERE."

With that, Teggs stamped on the brakes, and the space-sleigh stopped dead!

Loki squawked as he tried to steer past it — and if he hadn't been pulling such a large carriage behind him, he might just have been able to. Instead, the carriage clanged into the back of the brand-new vessel, giving Teggs and Iggy a nasty knock. And the impact sent Loki's space-sleigh completely out of control!

"I'll get you one day, Teggs!"
bellowed Loki, spinning helplessly
towards a pale-brown planet. "Just you
wait . . ."

"I won't hold my breath!" Teggs
shouted.

"But if I were Loki, I *would* hold my
nose!" said Iggy, tapping

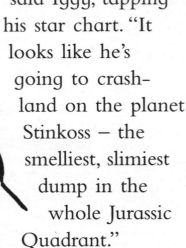

his star chart. "It
looks like he's
going to crash-
land on the planet
Stinkoss — the
smelliest, slimiest
dump in the
whole Jurassic
Quadrant."

"He and his raptor army should fit
in very well!" Teggs beamed. "Has our
sleigh been damaged?"

"Dented and scratched, but otherwise
OK," said Iggy. "Which is more than
you can say for the raptor fleet!"

122

"Then let's get back to Exmus and join the others," said Teggs. "I feel as if all my Christmases have come at once – which means we've got some *serious* celebrating to do!"

Chapter Eleven

A CHRISTMAS TO REMEMBER

It was close to midnight on Christmas
Eve when Teggs and Iggy touched down
again in the parking bay on Exmus. All
the snow and ice had been cleared, and
Gipsy and Arx were waiting by the
entrance to the grotto with big smiles on
their faces.

"Sprite just signalled us with the good
news," said Arx. "He watched the battle
on the long-range scanner. Those
satellites you took with you wiped out
half the raptor invasion force – and the
other half ran away!"

"We've already called Admiral Rosso
at DSS HQ and told him to send a

dozen ultra-secure prison ships to Stinkoss," Gipsy added. "So Loki and his army will be well taken care of – together with Ranpak and his buddies in the workshop."

"Good!" said Teggs. "How about Papa Claws? Is he all right?"

Arx smiled and pointed to the night sky with his horns.

Teggs looked up and saw a space-sleigh towing hundreds of carriages, slowly disappearing into the starry distance.

"Papa Claws!" he yelled at the top of his lungs. "I've always wanted to know – why *do* you deliver all those gifts every year?"

"Because it's ridiculous!" Papa Claws shouted back. "Because I love Christmas! And because . . . it's just *fun*!"

With the faintest jingling of bells, the space-sleigh sped out of sight.

"Well, it was touch-and-go and a lot of hard work," said Nickel, as he and Hans came out to join the astrosaurs in the parking bay. "But Papa Claws *just* got away in time to deliver all his presents."

"Christmas is saved!" Hans cheered. "Loki couldn't spoil it, however hard he tried."

"No one can spoil Christmas," Teggs agreed quietly, "because it's the most special day in the universe."

Even as he spoke, the clocks in the grotto chimed twelve.

"And now it's here!" cried Arx. "Christmas is *here*!"

"It's ho-ho-HERE," sang Hans and Nickel, as they did a little celebration jig. "It's oh-so ho-ho-HERE!"

"Merry Christmas, everyone!" hooted Gipsy. She hugged Arx and Iggy, and planted a big kiss on the end of Teggs's nose. He blushed and hugged her back. "So far, it's been the craziest Christmas *ever*."

Teggs grinned. "And I can't ever remember enjoying one more!"

"Come on, you lot!" Nickel was smiling, his cheeks red and rosy. "We must help the other elfosaurs get ready for the big celebration when Papa Claws comes back."

Gipsy frowned. "But won't he be really tired?"

"Ha!" said Hans. "It's not the delivering presents that wears him out – it's the big party we have afterwards!"

"I'll have me a piece of that!" Iggy grinned. "Tell you what, I'll even make another of my extra-sticky Christmas puds!"

"Can we bring everyone from on board the *Sauropod*?" asked Arx.

"Of course," Nickel told him. "The more the merrier!"

"Parrrr-tayyyy!" Gipsy cheered.

"And let's hope that Papa Claws brings us a sleigh-load of new adventures for Christmas," said Teggs. "Enough to last us right the way through the happy New Year!"

THE END

A CHRISTMAS CHALLENGE

Papa Claws bought each of the astrosaurs a special present – but for a bit of fun, he decided to scramble up their names on the labels.

Arx worked out whose gift was whose in 1.2 seconds. See if you can unscramble these anagrams in under two minutes. Good luck – and CHAMMY STIRRERS!

AXON ROAR
EASY UPRISING
GOAT GANGSTER SPACESUIT
TOOTHY GIG

And can you guess what "Chammy Stirrers" means?